Provided

by

Measure B

which was approved

by the voters in

November, 1998

Amoo Norooz

and

Other Persian Stories

Amoo Norooz

and

Other Persian Stories

The Tale of Ringy

The Crystal Flower and the Sun

Bastoor

Compiled and Edited by
AHMAD K. JABBARI

Mazda Publishers, Inc.
Costa Mesa, California U.S.A.
2000

Mazda Publishers, Inc.
P.O. Box 2603
Costa Mesa, California 92626 U.S.A.
www.mazdapublishers.com

Library of Congress Cataloging-in-Publication Data

Amoo Norooz and Other Persian Stories/compiled and edited by Ahmad Jabbari
p. cm
English and Persian.
Contents: Amoo Norooz—The Tale of Ringy—The Crystal Flower and the Sun—Bastoor.

ISBN: 1-56859-065-2
(Hardcover, alk. paper)

1. Folklore—Iran. 2. Persian language materials—Bilingual.
I. Ahmad K. Jabbari, 1945-
PZ90.P4A66 1997 and 2000
398.2'0955—dc21
97-34550
CIP
AC NE

CONTENTS

Editor's Note

These four stories were first published in separate volumes in 1983. They were widely received among the growing number of Persian immigrants and their American friends. The books were quickly sold out and had remained out of print until now when I decided to combine them into one convenient volume.

Amoo Norooz is the story of the coming of the Persian new year, *Norooz*, which begins on the twenty-first of March, the first day of spring. *Norooz* is celebrated in Iran (Persia), Afghanistan, countires around the Persian Gulf, Turkey, parts of China, among the Parsi's in India, and some former Soviet Republics such as Tajikistan, Uzbakistan, and Azerbaijan, to name a few. Like Santa Clause, who symbolizes Christmas and New Year for the Christians, *Amoo Norooz* is the symbol of the New Year for the Persians and those nations who have been influenced by the Persian civilization throughout history. This is one of the oldest tales passed down from generation to generation, keeping the tradition of Persian New Year alive. Because of the importance of this story, I decided to present it in a bilingual format.

The Tale of Ringy, is the story of a young bird with a ring of feathers around his neck, and so the name "Ringy." In this story, which is told and translated in poetry style, Ringy learns a valuable lesson about team work. One morning Ringy finds a cotton boll and brings it to his father. Wondering what it is, he begins to peck on it in an attempt to break it open. His father tells him that indeed this cotton boll is used to make a gown. Seeing the astonished look on Ringy's face, he sends him off into the world to discover for himself how, by cooperation and division of tasks between the spinner, the weaver, the dyer, and the tailor, this cotton boll ultimately is turned into a gown. This story teaches children the true meaning of societal cooperation between its members.

The Crystal Flower and the Sun is an original story written by Fardideh Farjam. This story was awarded a prize by the National Commission of Unesco in Japan in 1970. The story is about friendship and coexistence between two diametrically opposite elements; one made of frozen water, and the other the source of energy for all living things on our planet. But when there is respect for one another, the story teaches us, even these two elements can live in peace and harmony side-by-side without the stronger one, the Sun, melting the weaker one, the Crystal Flower.

Bastoor is a stirring tale for children inspired by a passage in the ancient epic of Iran (Persia), the *Shahnameh*, or *The Epic of the Kings*, written by the poet Ferdowsi in tenth-century. In translating and adapting *Bastoor* for English-speaking children and young readers, every effort was made to keep faithfully to the epic tone and style of the author's original version. However, a few changes in the text itself were considered necessary. For example, proper names have been simplified, some obscure references to Iranian (Persian) mythology have been omitted, and the original story has been condensed. Such adaptations were minor, but will increase the reader's appreciation of this story of a young boy who takes the place of his fallen father in the battlefield. His bravery results in the saving of Iranian independence from foreign invaders.

I dedicate this volume to my children, Parsa and Shiva, and to their cousins, Sina and Sanaz.

Ahmad K. Jabbari
Irvine, California

Amoo Norooz

Story by Farideh Farjam and Meyer Azaad

Illustrations by Farsheed Mesqali

Translated from the Persian by Ahmad K. Jabbari

Once upon a time there was a man named Amoo Norooz.
Every year on the first day of spring Amoo Norooz, wearing a felt
hat, his hair and beard dyed red with henna, and wearing a blue
sash, baggy dark-blue pants, and shoes made of heavy cotton
yarn, walked to the city with a cane in his hand.

یکی بود یکی نبود، غیر از خدا هیچ‌کس نبود. مردی بود به‌اسم عمونوروز. هرسال اول

بهار عمونوروز با کلاهِ نمدی، ریش و زلف حنابسته، کمرچینِ آبی، شلوارِ گشادِ سرمه‌ای

و گیوهٔ تختِ نازکِ مِلکی، عصا زنان به‌شهر می‌آمد.

Outside the gates of the city lay a small beautiful garden. Every kind of Fruit the heart desired could be found in the garden. Many bushes bursting with flowers grew in the garden. Every year at the beginning of spring pink and white blossoms covered the branches on the trees.

بیرون دروازهٔ شهر، باغ کوچک قشنگی بود. توی این باغ هر جور میوه‌ای که دلت می‌خواست پیدا می‌شد. و فراوان بوته‌های پُر گل داشت ! هرسال اول بهار شاخه‌های درخت‌ها پر از شکوفه می‌شد: شکوفه‌های صورتی، شکوفه‌های سفید.

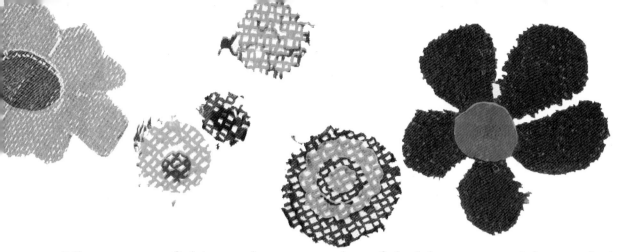

The owner of this garden was a cheerful old woman with gray hair. The old woman liked Amoo Norooz very much. Each year on the first day of spring she woke up early in the morning, made her bed, washed her hands and face, and said her morning prayers. She then swept out her room, brought out her pretty silken rug, and spread it on the veranda. Next she watered the flowers in the garden across from the veranda. All around the garden's edge were planted seven bushes of flowers of seven different colors—narcissus, marigotd, bushes of flowers of seven different colors—narcissus, marigotd, pansy, red rose, tulip, iris and morning glory.

صاحب این باغچهٔ کوچک پیرزن سفیدموی خوش‌رویی بود. پیرزن عمو نوروز را خیلی دوست داشت. هر سال روز اول بهار، صبح زود از خواب بیدار می‌شد. رختخوابش را جمع می‌کرد، وضو می‌گرفت و نماز می‌خواند. اتاق را جارو می‌کرد. قالیچهٔ ابریشمی قشنگش را می‌آورد توی ایوان پهن می‌کرد. و باغچهٔ روبروی ایوان را آب‌پاشی می‌کرد. دور تا دور باغچه هفت بوتهٔ گل هفت‌رنگ بود: نرگس و همیشه‌بهار، بنفشه و گل سرخ، لاله و زنبق و نیلوفر.

In front of the garden was a tiled pool. A few fish of
different colors swam playfully in the pool.

جلوی باغچه یک حوض کاشی بود. توی این حوض چندتا ماهی رنگارنگ
شنا می‌کردند.

The old woman turned on the fountain that flowed from the middle of the pool. The fountain sprinkled sparkling drops of water covering the flowers and the bushes in the garden. Then she brought out her silver-rimmed mirror and sat down on the rug. She combed and braided her hair, darkened her eyelashes with mascara, and rubbed rouge on her cheeks. Over her silk dress she put on a vest of silk brocade and wore a scarf. She sprayed rose water on her hair and lit a stick of aloes wood.

پیرزن می‌رفت سرِ حوضِ فوّاره را باز می‌کرد. آب برق برق می‌زد و روی گل‌ها و بوته‌ها

می‌ریخت. آن‌وقت می‌رفت و آینهٔ پایه‌دارِ نقره‌اش را می‌آورد و روی قالیچه می‌نشست.

Then she lit a fire in the brazier, placed a velvet pouch of incense next to it, and brought out the water pipe. In the crystal vase of the water pipe she laid a few rose petals.

In several crystal dishes she arranged seven different kinds of cookies, candies, and sweets and laid them down beside the *haftsin,* a tray containing seven different kinds of foods whose names all began with the letter "S." Finally she sat on the rug to wait for Amoo Norooz to arrive.

موهایش را شانه می‌زد و می‌بافت. چشم‌هایش را سُرمه می‌کشید. لُپ‌هایش را گُلی می‌کرد .
روی پیراهن تافته‌اش نیم‌تنهٔ زَری می‌پوشید و چارقد زری سر می‌کرد. گلاب به‌موهایش می‌زد.
عود روشن می‌کرد. منقل آتش را درست می‌کرد. کیسهٔ مخمل اسفند را کنار منقل می‌گذاشت.
توی کوزهٔ قلیان بلوری چندتا برگ گل می‌انداخت. بعد سینی هفت‌سین را می‌آورد روی قالیچه می‌گذاشت.
تو چند ظرف بلور، هفت جور شیرینی و نقل و نبات می‌چید و پهلوی هفت‌سین می‌گذاشت
و می‌نشست روی قالیچه و منتظر عمو نوروز می‌شد.

Slowly the old woman's eyelids grew heavy and she started to doze. Soon she was asleep, dreaming about meeting Amoo Norooz. At the moment the old woman fell asleep, Amoo Norooz entered the garden. He saw her asleep and smiling in her dreams.

پیرزن کم کم خوابش می‌گرفت، چُرت می‌زد، پلک‌هایش سنگین می‌شد، بخواب می‌رفت و عمونوروز را خواب می‌دید. در این‌میان عمونوروز سر می‌رسید، می‌دید پیرزن خوابش برده و توی خواب لبخند می‌زند.

Amoo Norooz did not have the heart to awaken her. Instead, he picked a marigold from the garden and gently tucked it in the old woman's gray hair.

عمو نوروز دلش نمی‌آمد پیرزن را از خواب بیدار کند. یک گل همیشه‌بهار را از باغچه می‌چید و به‌موهای سفید پیرزن می‌زد.

Then he took an orange
from the tray and cut it
in half with a knife.
One-half he ate with
some sugar and water,
and the other half he left
for the old woman.

نارنج سفرهٔ هفت‌سین را برمی‌داشت با چاقو نصف می‌کرد. نصفش را
با قند و آب می‌خورد، و نصف دیگرش را هم برای پیرزن می‌گذاشت.
یک‌مشت اسفند از توی کیسهٔ مخمل در می‌آورد و روی آتش می‌ریخت.

He took out some incense from the velvet pouch and burned it in the fire. The pieces of the incense burned noisily in the fire, filling the air with a sweet smell. Using a few red-hot coal from the brazier, he lit the water pipe. After a few smokes, he got up and left the garden to take the New Year to the city.

اسفندها می‌پریدند هوا ترق و توروق صدا می‌کردند. بوی اسفند در هوا می‌پیچید. عمو نوروز چند گل آتش هم روی سرِ قلیان می‌گذاشت. قلیان را چاق می‌کرد، چند پُکی به قلیان می‌زد و آن وقت پا می‌شد و می‌رفت تا عید را به شهر ببرد.

The sun slowly rose above the treetops, filling the garden and reaching the veranda. It shone on the old woman's face, waking her up. She rubbed her eyes, saw the halfeaten orange Amoo Norooz had left behind, and smelled the incense.

"I have missed him again," she cried. "The year has changed, but I did not see Amoo Norooz because I fell asleep again."

آفتاب کم کم از سر درخت‌ها پایین می‌آمد، در حیاط پهن می‌شد، به ایوان می‌رسید .

و می‌افتاد روی صورت پیرزن . پیرزن از خواب می‌پرید، چشم‌هایش را می‌مالید، تا

نارنج نصف‌شده را می‌دید. و بوی اسفند به دماغش می‌خورد، شستش خبردار می‌شد که :

« ای دل غافل ! دیدی باز عمو نوروز آمد، عید را آورد، سال تحویل شد و من خواب

ماندم و ندیدمش . »

دستی به زلف‌هایش می‌کشید ،
گل همیشه‌بهار را از گوشهٔ
چارقدش در می‌آورد و می‌گفت :
« ای داد بیداد . بازهم باید یک
سال آزگار صبر کنم . »

She raised her hand to her hair and found a marigold tucked under her scarf. "Alas!" she said. "Now I must wait another full year again." And the old woman would wait another year until winter was gone and Amoo Norooz would arrive, along with the spring wind. She would wait to lay her anxious eyes on him because, according to the legend, whoever meets Amoo Norooz will stay young and fresh, like spring, forever.

No one knows whether the old woman ever saw Amoo Norooz. Perhaps one spring she will remain awake and meet him at last. Then, she will be as fresh and young as spring itself and take along spring into the city with Amoo Norooz.

و پیرزن یکسال دیگر هم صبر می کرد تا زمستان بسر بیاید. عمو نوروز همراه باد بهاری از راه برسد. و چشمهای پیرزن از دیدن عمو نوروز روشن شود. چون می گویند هر کسی که عمو نوروز را ببیند، تا دنیا دنیاست دنیا مثل بهار تر و تازه می ماند.

هیچ کس نمی داند آخرش پیرزن توانست عمو نوروز را ببیند یا نه؟ شاید یکسال، موقع تحویل، پیرزن بیدار بماند. عمو نوروز را ببیند و جوان و تر و تازه بشود. و همراه عمو نوروز عید را بهشهر ببرد.

The Tale of RINGY

Story by Meyer Azaad

Illustrations by Nahid Haqiqat

Translated by M. R. Ghanoonparvar
and Diane L. Wilcox

Once upon a far-off time
In a place far away
There was a pretty little bird
So beautiful and gay
When he flew, his feathers
Turned to green and blue
Like the colors of the rainbow
With bright yellow and red, too.
Chirp, chirp, chirp
He would always sing
With no other music
His voice would ring
On the trees
In the breeze
On the bushes
In the bushes

This side of the brook
That side of the brook
Here, there, and everywhere
Our pretty, pretty little bird
Our happy, short-legged little bird
Had around his long, proud neck

A lovely, bright red ring
That was there for all to see
Whenever he would sing.
The children took one look at him
And stopped their merry game
They decided then and there
That Ringy was his name.
One spring morning
One fine day
With sky of blue
And flowers so gay
Sunshine and moonshine
Red and white
The moon grew pale
As the sun shone bright
O'er the horizon
The moon did run
As behind the mountain
Rose Lady Sun

The good news cock
Crowed at dawn
Flapped his wings
And jumped o'er the lawn
Quick and nimble
He jumped on the roof
Bing, bang, boom
Huff, puff, poof
Cock-a-doodle-doo
Cock-a-doodle-doo
Who's asleep?
And who's awake?

Rise and shine, Ringy dear
Get to work, for goodness sake.
Little Ringy
Woke with a start
Rubbed his eyes
And to the pool did dart
Splashed his face
And returned to his place.

Ringy and his papa
Set out to go
Through the fields
To and fro
Looking for seeds
Through grass and weeds
Ringy gleefully jumped over here
Ringy gleefully jumped over there
Picking up seeds from everywhere
He walked and walked and walked
He jumped and jumped and jumped
He ran and ran and ran.
Swish, swish, swish
Blew the mighty wind
And from the cotton field
A tiny cotton boll
falling from the air
On the ground did roll
The boll rolled and rolled
To where Ringy could see
And he said to himself:
"What could this be?"

(He plucked up the boll
And to his papa did run)
"What is this, Papa?
Can I eat one?"
(He pecked on the boll)
"It doesn't taste good!"
His papa then laughed:
"And who says it should?"
He laughed and laughed
"No, Ringy my sweet,
This is a cotton boll
Not something to eat."
"Then what is it for?"
"Well, listen to me,
It is something to wear."
"But how can that be?"
"I'll tell you how
And then you will see:
They plant cotton seeds
And water them well
Till they grow to a bush
Very large, you can tell

On each cotton bush
At least ten branches grow
Then go to the dyer
For color and hue
And on every branch
Many bolls high and low.
Now, Ringy dear,
Go take a stroll
Into the village

With your cotton boll
To take to the spinner
To spin your yarn
Then make it to cloth
At the weaver's shop, too,

Then go to the dyer
For color and hue
Then the tailor will make
New Year clothing for you."
Now, Master Ringy
Flew up to the sky
Flapping his wings
Until, by and by
He'd passed over fields
And the mountain top
Straight to the village
To the spinner's shop.

Mr. Spinner, working hard
Spinning yarn, began to sing
With no other music
His voice did ring:
"Spin, spin my little spindle
Turn, little wheel, turn all day
Spinning yarn from cotton bolls
From Monday morn to Saturday
On Sunday, I travel about
Through the fields or sit on a rock."

Ringy flew up to the door
Knock, knock, knock
"Mr. Spinner, I have cotton
Will you spin it up for me?"
"Why, of course, I'll spin it, sir
And very nicely, you will see."
"If you spin the cotton
Into yarn for me
How much will you charge?
How much will that be?"
      Mr. Spinner stared at him
      And raising up his head
      He unknit his wrinkled brow
      And with a laugh he said:
      "My little sir
      My little son
      My pudgy, wudgy little one
      Listen to what I have to say

Listen to the song I sing
With no other music
My voice will ring."
To the spinner, Ringy said:
"Mr. Spinner, sing me a song
With no other music
just sing along
Sing it pretty
Sing it sweet
Louder, louder
Keep that beat.

(No matter how much time you spend
The work you have will never end!)"
"I've got the spindle
If your cotton is set
I'll do the spinning
And yarn you will get
I'll work for three days
You have money in your sash
If you want me to spin
You can pay me in cash."
"Oh, Mr. Spinner,"
Little Ringy did say,
"I have no sash
So how can I pay?"
"Don't worry," the spinner
Then said with a laugh,
"Just take the cotton

And divide it in half
Divide one half
Again in two
Half for my wages
The rest for you
No more, no less
No less, no more
If you don't agree
Shoo, out the door!"
Ringy was pleased
And so he agreed:
"Start spinning the cotton
And take what you need."

And so the spinner
Spun with care
The yarn for Ringy
And took his share.
Ringy took the yarn
And flew away
To the weaver's shop
That very day.
As the weaver wove
He would sing
With no other music
His voice would ring:

"Weave and weave
My little loom
Weave with me
In my little room
Knot the weft to the warp
Weave the cloth for me
I work and work all day long
The end to work I'll never see.
Little Ringy flew and flew
Till he reached the weaver's door:
Knock, knock, knock, knock
Then he knocked no more.
"Hello, Mr. Weaver, sir
Cloth is what I need
I have brought this yarn to weave
If you are agreed."
Mr. Weaver laughed and spoke
As kindly as could be:
"Why, of course I'll weave it, sir
And very nicely, you will see."

"If you weave the cotton yarn
Into cotton cloth for me
How much will you charge for this?
How much will that be?"
Mr. Weaver sang:

"My little sir
My little son
My pudgy, wudgy little one
Listen to what I have to say
Listen to the song I sing

With no other music
My voice will ring."
"Mr. Weaver
Sing a song
With no other music
Just sing along
Sing it pretty
Sing it sweet

Louder, louder
Keep that beat
(No matter how much
　　time you spend
The work you have
　　will never end)."
The warp is yours
The comb is mine
The weft is yours
The work is mine
You have the yarn
And money in your sash
I'll do the work
If you pay me in cash."
"Oh, Mr. Weaver,"
Little Ringy did say,
"I have no sash
So how can I pay?"
"Don't worry," the weaver
Then said with a laugh
"Just take the yarn
And divide it in half

Divide one half
Again in two
Half for my wages
The rest for you."
Ringy was pleased
And so he agreed
And then Mr. Weaver
Went to work with speed.
Ringy happily took the cloth
Straight to the dyer's door:
Knock, knock, knock, knock
And then he knocked no more.
"Hello, Mr. Dyer, sir."
"And how do you do;
Little Master Ringy,
What can I do for you?"
"I have some cloth
For you to dye
In pretty colors
Like the clear blue sky
Or leaves of green
Or a butterfly.
Mr. Dyer, if you dye
This cotton cloth for me
How much will you charge?

How much will that be?"
Then the dyer
Said with a laugh:
"Just take the cloth
And divide it in half
Divide one half
Again in two
Half for my wages
The rest for you
No more, no less
No less, no more
If you don't agree
Shoo, out the door!"
Ringy was pleased
And so he agreed:
"Start dying the cloth
And take what you, need."
Mr. Dyer went to work
With the colors he'd use
And dyed Ringy's cloth
In seven lovely hues.

Happily, Ringy took the cloth
To the tailor, who loved to sing
With no other music
His voice would ring:
"My needle sews and sews and sews
My needle is my friend
I make stitches all day long
But my work will never end."
Knock, knock, knock, knock
"Mr. Tailor, sir, hello
I have brought some cloth with me
That I'd like for you to sew."
"Why, of course I'll sew it, sir
And very nicely, you will see."
"How much will you charge for this?
How much will that be?"
"My little sir
My little son
My pudgy, wudgy little one
Listen to what I have to say
Listen to the song I sing
With no other music

My voice will ring."
"Mr. Tailor
Sing me a song
With no other music
Just sing along
Sing it pretty
Sing it sweet

Louder, louder
Keep that beat
(No matter how much time you spend
The work you do will never end)."
"Mine are the scissors,
The needle, the thread
Yours are the sweets

And the parties ahead.
I'll work for three days
You have money in your sash
If you want me to sew
You can pay me in cash."
    "Oh, Mr. Tailor,"
    Little Ringy did say,
    "I have no sash
    So how can I pay?"
    "Don't worry," the tailor
    Then said with a laugh
    Just take the cloth

And divided it in half
Divide one half
Again in two
Half for my wages
The rest for you
No more, no less
No less, no more
If you don't agree
Shoo, out the door!"
Ringy was pleased
And so he agreed
And then Mr. Tailor
Worked with speed
Upon a lovely little robe
For little Ringy dear
One that he'd be proud to wear
To celebrate the New Year
And what a beautiful robe it was
One of many hues

One of many, many colors
Spring greens and ocean blues.
Our pretty, pretty little bird
With his short legs and colorful ring
And his long, proud neck
Stretched to sing
This bird of birds
On New Year's day
Put on his robe
And went to play
The children took one look at him
And stopped their merry game
They decided then and there
That Ringy was his name.

The Crystal Flower and the Sun

Story by Farideh Farjam
Illustrated by Nikzad Nojoomi
Translated from the Persian by Ahmad K. Jabbari

Night filled the sky of the North Pole. The night stayed one month, two months, three months, she stayed six full months. Then she began to fall asleep. The stars blinked so much that they too dimmed out.

"I am freezing," said the moon.

The night, the moon, and the stars vanished one by one.

In faraway lands, the sun rose over the crowded cities and green plains. He traveled and traveled until he reached the North Pole. It was day.

The sun was orange in color. His orange rays shone over the ice and snow. The Sun leaned on the blue wall of the sky and mused to himself, "What a quiet world this is!"

He then put his hands under his chin and watched. The sky was cold and the earth frozen as far as the eyes could see. A white bird flew off from the beach of the sea of ice and gleamed in the sun's rays. Up in the sky the rainbow, like seven silken ribbons, had seven colors.

And time passed.
The sun saw pieces of ice sparkle in his rays, make "chinkle-chinkle" sounds, crack, let loose of their grips, and separate. Slowly, a lone branch of icicle pushed her head out.

Leaves of clean pieces of ice sprouted from around the branch, snowflakes clung to it, and a crystal flower grew tall before the sun. The rainbow bent down and reached out to touch the crystal flower. The colors stuck to the crystal flower, turning her into a rainbow of colors.

The sun in his journey of thousands and thousands of years had seen many flowers—flowers with large petals and flowers with tiny petals. He had seen blue, pink, purple, and white flowers, but never before had he seen a crystal flower.

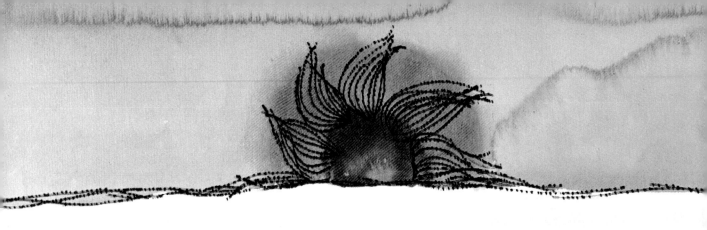

"Greetings, crystal flower," said the sun.

"Greetings," replied the crystal flower, sparkling.

Weeks passed and the sun could not take his eyes off the crystal flower.

One day the sun said to the crystal flower, "Tell me, how did you grow from the midst of the ice?"

"When you arrived in our land," replied the crystal flower, "I saw your light from behind the ice and followed your rays to come out of the ice."

"If people had seen you, they would have picked you and placed you in a vase in a room," said the sun.

"Tell me," asked the crystal flower, "do flowers grow everywhere you shine?"

The sun wanted to set and leave the answer until the next day. But the sun does not set each day at the North Pole. When he arrives, he must stay for six months. So the sun replied, "In other places the flowers pull themselves out from under the earth and live in my light. All around them the air is fresh. Their stems and leaves come alive and flutter in cool breezes."

"Then why," asked the crystal flower, "is my stem stuck to ice? Why does nothing move around me?"

"Can't you see," replied the sun, "that all around you as far as the eyes can see is frozen?"

And so the sun spoke to the crystal flower for days and days. He told her of all he had seen in the world—of the wheat fields that grow by the hillside, of the young shepherd boys who tend the herd of sheep, of the villagers who plant the fields, and of gardens full of fruits and flowers. The sun told the crystal flower of the people in the cities who rushed to work and of the wondrous things workers made in the factories.

The sun spoke and spoke and spoke until months had passed. The day arrived when the sun had to leave the North Pole.

The crystal flower asked, "Sun, why are you gathering your rays?"

The sun answered, "I must gather up my rays, one by one, and return to the other lands where trees, birds, and people are all waiting for the morning."

The crystal flower said, "If you leave, the night will come. It will be dark, and I will not be able to see anything."

The sun was sad. He turned blue with sorrow and rested his head on the blue wall of the sky. The crystal flower cried out, "Sun! Sun! Take me with you! Pick me and put me in a vase in your room."

"You and I have been friends all the six months of light at the pole," said the sun. "Now I must leave. All my friends in the cities, fields, and villages depend on me to stay alive."

"I, too, want to see greater lands," replied the crystal flower, "the people who plant the fields, the villagers who water the farms and make the gardens full of flowers."

"If you come with me," said the sun, "you will melt and will no longer be a crystal flower. Now you are very faraway from me, and all of my heat does not reach you."

"I will not melt," replied the crystal flower. "I want to go with you to take light to your friends."

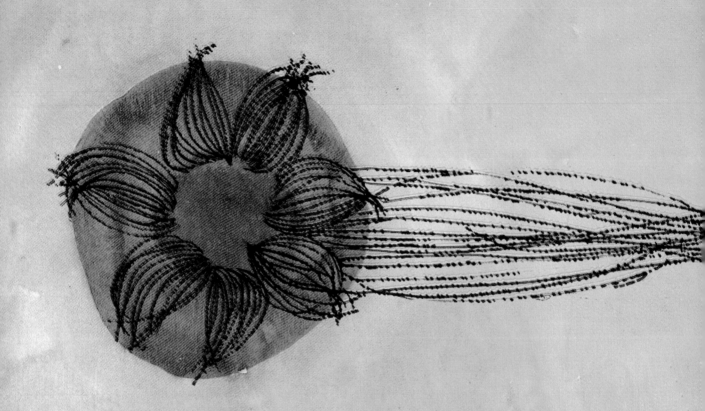

So the sun sent his rays towards the ice. The rays shone and shone until they reached the crystal flower. And, like a golden belt, they wrapped themselves around the crystal flower, clipping her free from the ice.

The sun said, "Let us go." And he rolled and rolled and rolled, passing over the mountains of ice until he reached the rocky

mountains, the fields, and the villages.

Near the cities the crystal flower said, "Sun, take me higher up and tuck me to your chest." The sun pulled her higher and said, "You will melt any minute now."

"It does not matter," replied the crystal flower. "I will bring the morning to all the people."

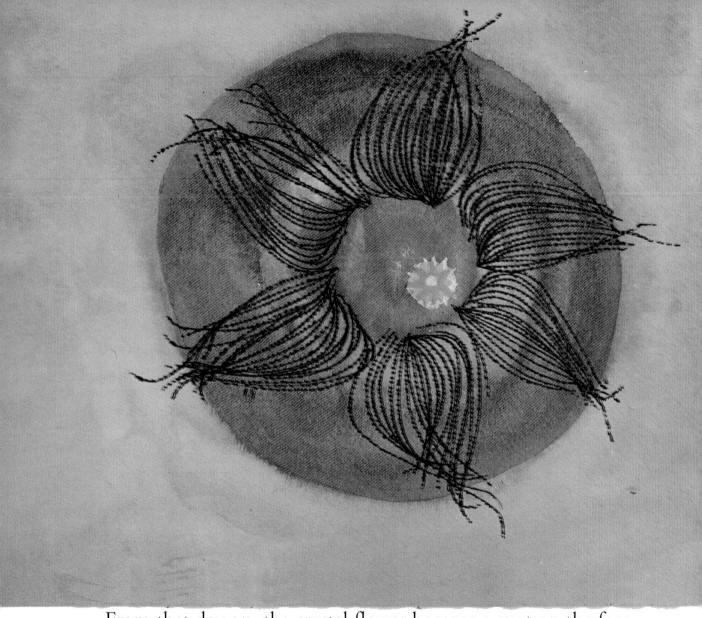

From that day on, the crystal flower became a spot on the face of the sun. See how she and the sun together bring morning and light to people all over the world.

Bastoor

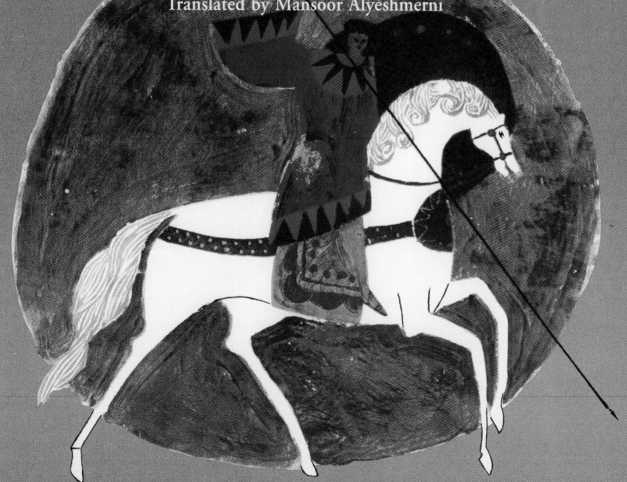

Story by Mehrdad Bahar
Illustrations by Nikzad Nojoomi
Translated by Mansoor Alyeshmerni

*L*ong, long ago, the Persians and the Turans were bitter enemies. They fought many battles and lost many battles and lost many brave men whose names are forgotten. But no one has forgotten the battle which took place in a wide valley between two high mountains—the famous battle won by a young Persian boy named Bastoor.

Horses, chariots, elephants, and the lances and shields of soldiers covered the slopes of both mountains. The trumpeting of elephants, the blare of bugles, the neighing of horses, and the songs and shouts of soldiers shook the earth and sky. At the top of one mountain sat Goshtep, the king of Persia, and all Persian chieftains. On the other mountain, King Jasseb of the Turans sat on a throne with the Turan chieftains gathered around him. The armies of the two kings faced each other across the valley.

Bastoor's father, Zarri, was a fierce warrior and the commander of the Persian army. To prepare for battle that day, Zarri removed his violet cloak, put on his chain mail and an iron helmet, and took up his steel sword and a long lance. Finally, he kissed the ground in front of King Goshtep as all heroes did before going into battle. Then, mounting his great white horse, he pulled upon its reins. The horse reared on its hind legs, neighed, then galloped down the mountain toward the scene of battle in the valley. Amidst all the dust kicked up by his horse, the tall warrior looked as though he were flying in a cloud.

When he came near the Turan army, Zarri shouted, "Who among you will fight me?" No one in the Turan army spoke up. All was silent. Then Zarri yelled out again, "Is there no one?" His loud shout echoed in the mountains and valley—NO-ONE-NO-ONE?

The king of the Turans feared that his people would be defeated unless he could find a warrior who would face Zarri. He called to his chieftains, "Isn't there a Turan among you who can fight Zarri and overcome him?" But no one stepped forward or said a word. Then King Jasseb cried out, "Whoever kills Zarri will win the right to marry my beautiful daughter Saresta."

Suddenly Bedaraf, the wicked Turan wizard, stood up, took a few steps forward, bowed down to the king, and boasted loudly, "Please command them to saddle a horse for me. I can conquer the great Zarri easily, but I will conquer by my witchcraft, not by my strength at arms."

So King Jasseb commanded that a horse be saddled for him. Bedaraf, in front of all the Turan chieftains, changed himself by magic into an old, old man. Then the wizard mounted a horse and rode toward the Persian camp.

When he saw the feeble old man riding toward him, Zarri roared with laughter. "Now I know that the Turans are cowardly dogs. Aren't there any warriors left in the camp of the Turans? Must they send this ancient relic to fight the great Zarri?"

"O Magnificent Commander," said Bedaraf slyly. "What fool would send a broken old man to fight such a powerful hero? No one has sent me to fight you. I have only come to see for myself the great hero whom no one dares to fight."

Zarri had no wish to kill a broken old man. He turned his back to Bedaraf, faced the Turans, and shouted, "Are there no men left among you? Is this old bag of bones your last warrior?" As soon as Zarri turned, the evil Bedaraf pulled out a poisoned dagger he had hidden in his cloak, jumped suddenly, and plunged the dagger into Zarri's back.

Zarri let out a shriek of pain that echoed between the mountains. Then he fell to the ground. The great warrior could no longer hurl his lance into the sky. He could no longer shake the mountains with his yell. He could no longer gallop his horse across the valley and send a cloud of dust into the air. The dust settled. And all was silent.

All of the Persian army, including Zarri's young son Bastoor, saw their commander fall and the old man race back toward the Turan camp. King Goshtep gave a great shout, ordering the Persians to attack the Turans and avenge Zarri. But the Persians were afraid to fight now that their mighty leader had been killed. So the king cried out, "Whoever now will lead the Persians against the Turans and avenge the death of Zarri will be named commander of the Persian army and will marry my beautiful young daughter, Princess Homa."

Bastoor, the young son of Zarri, heard the king's promise and alone of all the Persians said, "I will fight the Turans. Saddle a horse for me, and I will go avenge my father's death."

But King Goshtep looked down upon Bastoor and said, "You are a brave boy, but you are still too young."

"O King," Bastoor cried. "I am as brave and fierce as any warrior in the Persian army. Did not my father himself teach me to ride a horse and to use a sword? Although I am young, I have the strength and skill of a grown man."

King Goshtep frowned. "No, Bastoor. Wait until you are a grown man to avenge your father's death. That will be soon enough to test your strength in battle."

Bastoor listened patiently to the king's advice. But after he had heard all that was said, he waited until the king was talking to the Persian chieftains. Then quickly and quietly he walked to his tent. He hid his small sword under his clothes. He threw his bow over his shoulder. Then he secretly went to the stables, to the groom of his father's horses.

Zarri's great white stallion was just returning to its stable. The horse's head was low and full of sorrow. Its back was reddened by Zarri's blood. Zarri's arrow quiver still hung on its side.

Bastoor ran to the horse and took its head in his arms and kissed it and said, "Oh, why is my father dead? Tell me, who killed my father?" The horse only shook its head sadly and slowly.

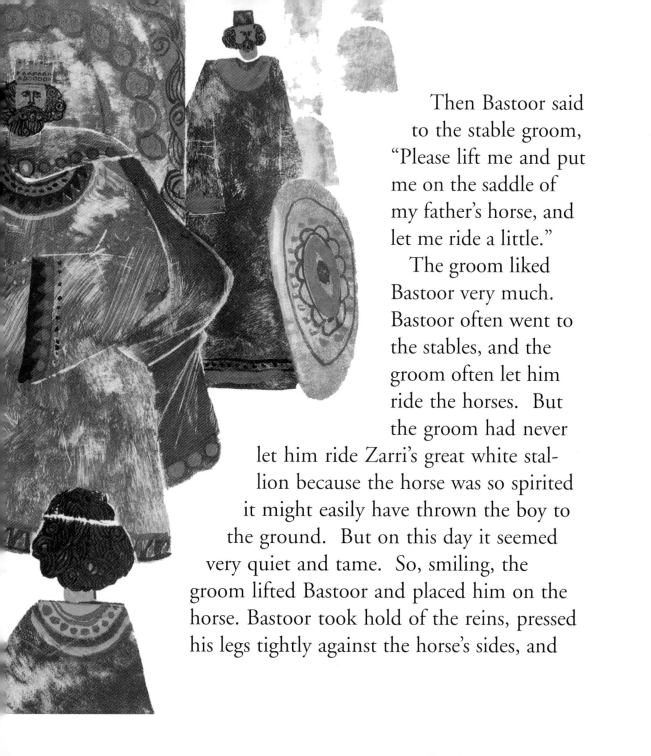

Then Bastoor said to the stable groom, "Please lift me and put me on the saddle of my father's horse, and let me ride a little."

The groom liked Bastoor very much. Bastoor often went to the stables, and the groom often let him ride the horses. But the groom had never let him ride Zarri's great white stallion because the horse was so spirited it might easily have thrown the boy to the ground. But on this day it seemed very quiet and tame. So, smiling, the groom lifted Bastoor and placed him on the horse. Bastoor took hold of the reins, pressed his legs tightly against the horse's sides, and

then bent down and whispered softly in its ear. "O beautiful white horse! I know you are sad. I know you are full of sorrow from the death of your rider. If you take me to the scene of this battle, I will avenge your master's death."

The horse reared with joy and neighed loudly. Bastoor started to fall, but he pulled on the reins and pressed his legs even more tightly against the horse. Then Bastoor swung his small sword into the air and shouted, "Forward to the scene of the battle!" The horse galloped down the mountain toward the scene of battle in the valley.

Bastoor's cry and the sound of the great stallion's gallop echoed between the mountains. King Goshtep and his chieftains were fearful and worried for the boy, and the king commanded that Bastoor be stopped. Two soldiers rode after Bastoor to bring him back. But it was too late.

When the Turan warriors first saw the small Persian boy charging across the field toward them, they laughed. But Zarri's great war horse was so angry that it kicked every Turan it came near. Then Bastoor would tear the enemy's chest with his small sword. The furious horse's hooves and the stroke of Bastoor's sword killed hundred of the Turan soldiers. Slowly Bastoor fought his way to where his father's body lay. Zarri had fallen on the ground, and his head and face were covered with dust.

Bastoor stopped suddenly and moaned. "O Father, why did you die? O Brave Man, who took your life? If only I could dismount and take you in my arms and remove the dust from your head and face.

"But I can do nothing. If I dismount, I will not be able to mount your horse again by myself and the Turans will come and kill me too." Sadly he turned away.

From atop the mountain King Jasseb saw Bastoor kill his strop warriors one after the other. Finally, no more soldiers would face Bastoor. They were truly afraid of Zarri's son. Fearfully, the king

turned to his chieftains and said, "Isn't there someone among you to fight this boy?" No one answered him. Then King Jasseb cried, "I promise great riches and the command of the Turan army to whoever will destroy this terrible boy warrior."

Once again, the wicked Bedaraf stepped forward and smiled craftily. "With my witchcraft, I can destroy the son as I destroyed the father." With those words, Bedaraf

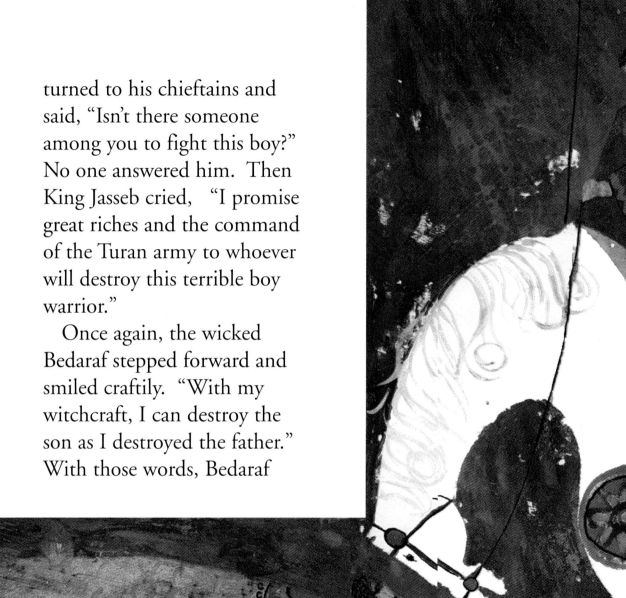

transformed himself into an old woman, an ugly crone. This time he hid the poisoned dagger in his wide skirt and then rode onto the battlefield.

Bastoor saw the ancient crone riding toward him on her black horse and laughed as his father had and asked, "Have you come to fight me, old hag?"

"Oh, no," said Bedaraf slyly. "What fool would send an old woman to fight a warrior? I have come to look at you because I have head there is no young man in all of Turan who is as powerful and handsome as you."

Bastoor believed her and did not have the heart to kill an old woman. Instead, he turned toward the Turans to mock them. "Have I already killed all your brave warriors? Can't you find a

man strong enough to fight me that you must send out an old hag?"

But as Bastoor spoke, Bedaraf craftily rode his horse around and behind the boasting boy. He pulled out the poisoned dagger and prepared to stab Bastoor as he had

Zarri. Suddenly Zarri's great war horse recognized the smell of the evil one. Rearing and snorting, the white stallion whirled to face Bedaraf. When Bastoor saw that Bedaraf the wizard was about to attack him, he took his bow from his shoulder, placed an arrow in it, and pulled the string tight. Bedaraf fled with

terror, but Zarri's horse followed him. Bastoor held on by pressing his legs against the horse's sides. With his hands he held the bow and arrow ready.

"Stop, coward!" Bastoor yelled out. "Are all Turans as cowardly as you? Treacherous old woman who is no woman, now I will avenge my father's death." And Bastoor let the arrow fly from his bow into the wizard's back. Bedaraf's cry of pain filled the skies. He dropped his dagger and fell off his horse.

The Turans wailed loudly and began to run away. Bastoor raised his sword high and, giving a loud war cry, charged after Turan army. When the Persians saw the Turans running away, they   followed their brave young leader with their horses and elephants.

By nightfall, the Turan army was completely defeated, and King Jasseb had fled. The next day the Persian army celebrated their victory from morning to night.

King Goshtep sat on his royal throne with his chieftains around him. Goshtep asked Bastoor to step forward and said, "Bastoor, you have won this battle for us. What would you like in return?"

Bastoor answered. "Only what you promised, O King. The command of the Persian army and the hand of the young   princess, your daughter."

All the chieftains laughed. Looking down at Bastoor, the king also laughed and said, "You are a brave boy, Bastoor, but you are still a boy. You must wait until you are a man before you can claim command of the Persian army and marry a princess."

Bastoor once more listened patiently to the king. But when he had heard all that was said, he spoke angrily. "I may be a boy, but I have fought better than all of you, and I am braver than all of you. Why can't I be rewarded like a man?" Then Bastoor ran away from Goshtep and his chieftains and went to his tent and threw himself onto his bed.

Bastoor was sad and unhappy, and he thought and thought. Why did he have to be a boy? Why wasn't he a tall grown man so that he could take command of the Persian army? Wasn't he braver than all the other warriors?

Bastoor began to cry, and as he cried he prayed to Hurmazda, the god of light. "O Hurmazda! Help me. Make me grow tall and strong quickly. Make me a man so that no one will laugh at me. Help me so that I may be rewarded as I deserve."

Then Bastoor fell asleep. But Hurmazda had heard his prayer.

Hours passed.

Bastoor awoke.

He saw that his hands had become larger.

He leaped up and stared at his legs. All of his body had grown. He did no believe it at first. He pinched himself and shook his legs to discover whether he was dreaming.

He was not dreaming. He had grown tall, tall, tall. He had become a man, handsome, tall, wide-shouldered—exactly like Zarri. Bastoor let out a loud whoop of joy and dashed out of the tent.

Goshtep and his chieftains were still celebrating. Bastoor walked among them and bowed down to the king and said, "Now do as you promised. I am a man."

At first the king and his chieftains were shocked and could not believe their eyes. But slowly Bastoor spoke to them and explained how his prayers to Hurmazda had been answered. When all the chieftains understood what had happened, they heered loudly for their new leader.

And so that same day Bastoor, son of Zarri, became commander of the Persian army and married the king's beautiful young daughter.